For SUSAN and PASCAL, C.M.
For ROBERT, H.R.

Many thanks to the staff and children at
Chalvey Nursery School and Assessment Unit,
and Salt Hill Nursery, Slough, Berkshire
for their help and advice.

Copyright © 2000 Zero to Ten Limited
Text copyright © 1996 Hannah Reidy
Illustrations copyright © 1996 Clare Mackie

Publisher: Anna McQuinn, Art Director: Tim Foster
Art Editor: Sarah Godwin, Designer: Suzy McGrath

First published in Great Britain in hardback in 1996
This edition published in 2000 by Zero to Ten Limited
327 High Street, Slough, Berkshire, SL1 1TX

A CIP catalogue record for this book is available from the British Library.

ISBN 1-84089-072-X
Printed in Hong Kong

Crazy Creature
Contrasts

Written by
Hannah Reidy

Illustrated by
Clare Mackie

This one is not, she's **sad**.

This creature is **slow**, he's last.

This one's not slow, she's **fast**.

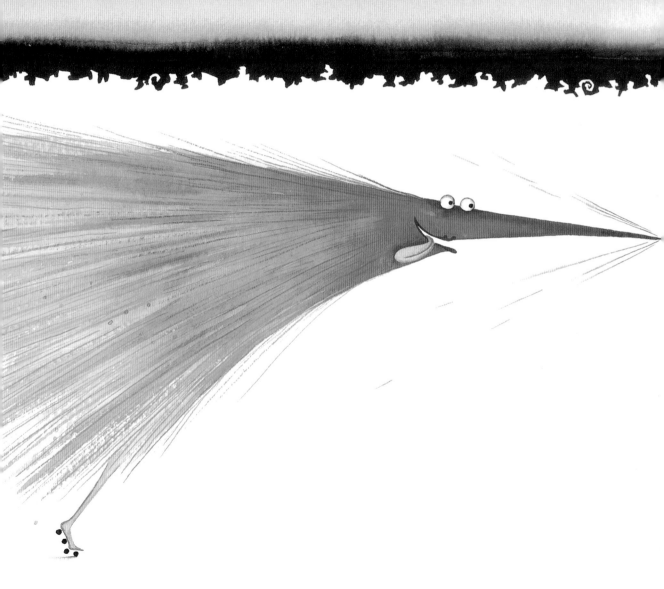

Yippee, his is **full!**

This creature is **hairy** all over.

This one is **hairless** and bare.

The **big** creature is caring and kind.

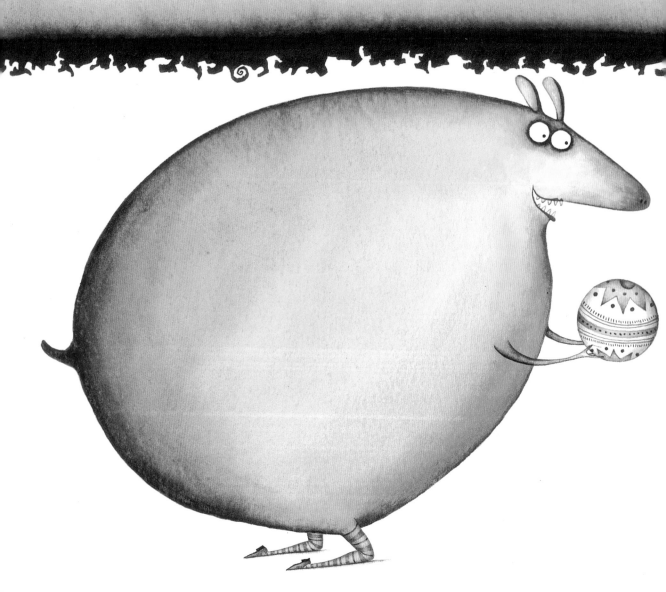

The little one is loving and giving.

This creature is content with a **few**.

This one's not, he's greedy for lots.

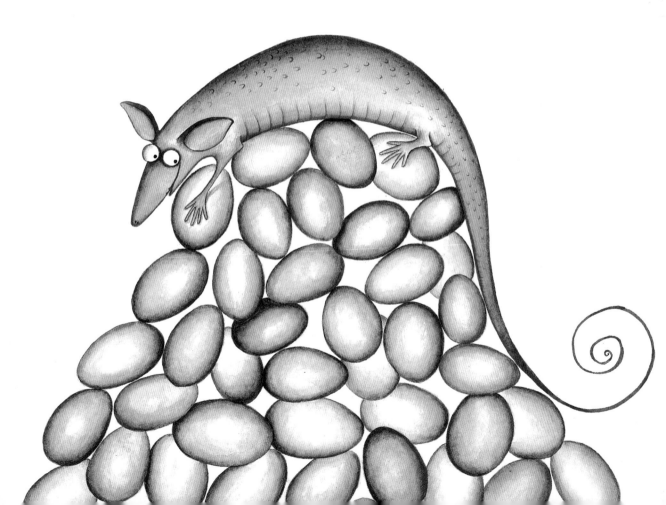

Oops! This creature is spotty.

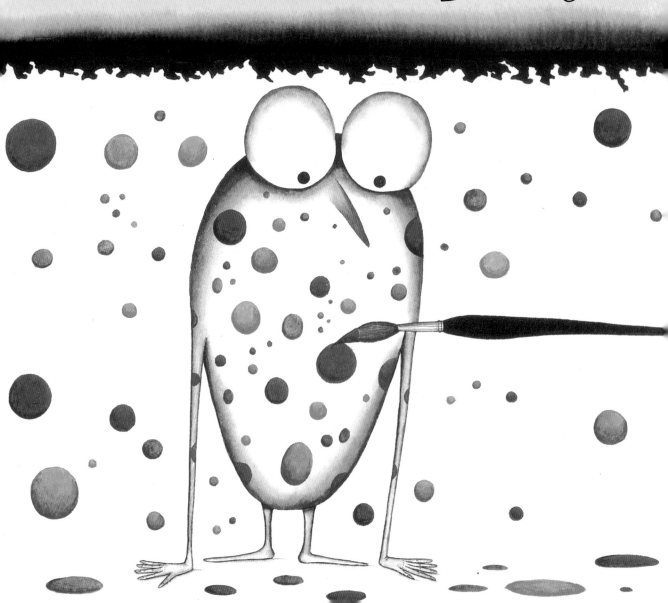

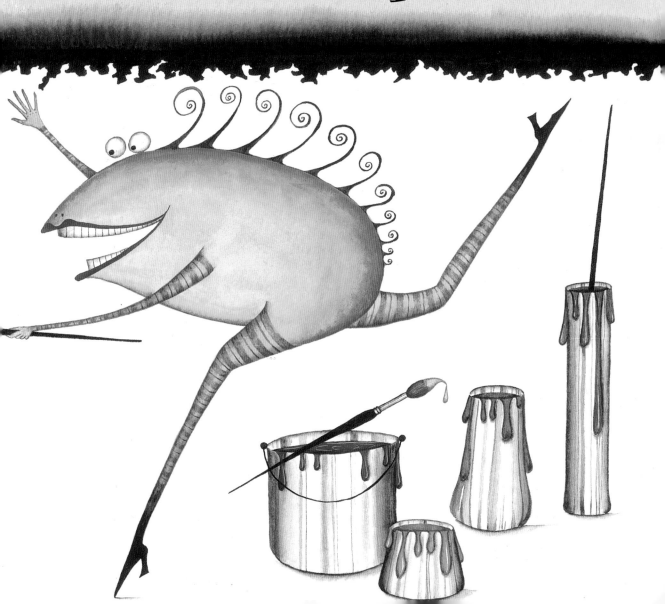

These creatures are dry...

and they're trying to get...

the other ones...

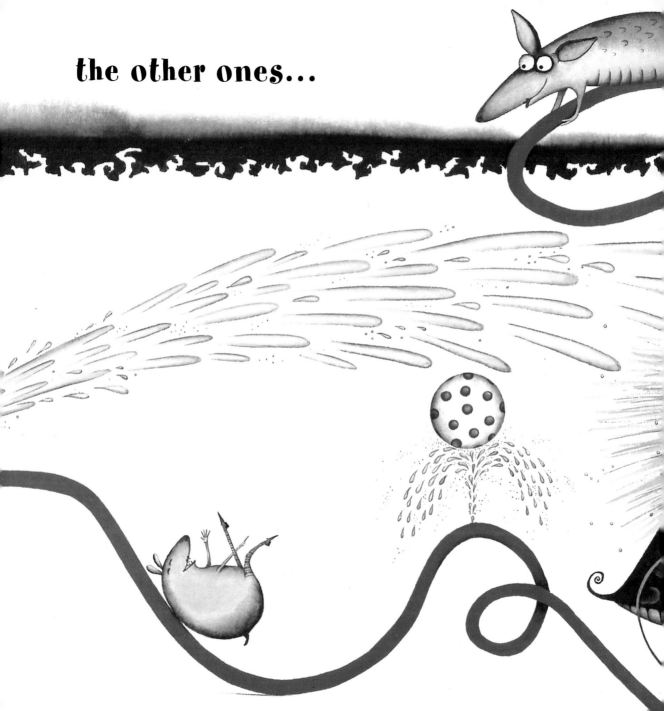